TOO
Small
Tola

Other books by Atinuke

For younger readers
Baby Goes to Market
illustrated by Angela Brooksbank

B Is for Baby
illustrated by Angela Brooksbank

Catch That Chicken!
illustrated by Angela Brooksbank

Hugo
illustrated by Birgitta Sif

Nonfiction
Africa, Amazing Africa: Country by Country
illustrated by Mouni Feddag

TOO
Small
Tola

ATINUKE

illustrated by
ONYINYE IWU

CANDLEWICK PRESS

Dedicated to Lani-Grace,
who is also small but mighty!

A

For Mum, Dad, Junior, Alessia, and Francis —
thanks for supporting my dreams.
This one is for you.

OI

Text copyright © 2020 by Atinuke
Illustrations copyright © 2020 by Onyinye Iwu

First US edition 2021
First published by Walker Books Ltd. (UK) 2020

Library of Congress Catalog Card Number pending
ISBN 978-1-5362-1127-6

20 21 22 23 24 25 LBM 10 9 8 7 6 5 4 3 2 1

Printed in Melrose Park, IL, USA

This book was typeset in Stempel Schneidler.
The illustrations were created digitally.

Candlewick Press
99 Dover Street
Somerville, Massachusetts 02144

www.candlewick.com

MIX
From responsible
sources
FSC® C103098

A JUNIOR LIBRARY GUILD SELECTION

CONTENTS

Dapo Grandmommy Moji

Tola

Too Small Tola

Tola lives in a run-down block of apartments in the megacity of Lagos, in the country of Nigeria. She lives with her sister, Moji, who is very clever; her brother, Dapo, who is very fast; and Grandmommy, who is very-very bossy.

Tola is the youngest in her family. And the smallest. And everybody calls her Too Small Tola, which makes her feel too-too small.

"Tola!" shouts Grandmommy. "O-ya, shopping! Let's go!"

Tola looks at Grandmommy in surprise. Shopping isn't her job! She is far too small to carry shopping!

"Why are you standing there looking at me?" asks Grandmommy. "Hurry up!"

"But . . ." Tola starts to argue.

She looks at her sister, Moji. Moji is big. Big enough to carry a mammy-wagon load of shopping.

But Moji is sitting at her borrowed computer doing her homework. She is wearing one of her A+ looks of concentration. Tola sighs. Everybody knows not to get in Moji's way when she is wearing that look.

What about her brother, Dapo? Dapo is fast. He could reach the market faster than an okada taxi.

But through the open window, carried on air as hot as pepper soup, come the sounds of boys playing football.

"Goal!" the boys roar. Then they start to chant, "Da-po! Da-po! Da-po!"

Tola sighs again. Everybody knows that Dapo is fantastic at football—and useless at everything else. Grandmommy says his tactics for avoiding work are as good as his football tactics.

Tola looks at Grandmommy. She is wearing one of her what-did-I-tell-you looks.

"Just hurry up, Tola," she says.

Tola hurries to put the big shopping basket on her head. She does not want to upset Grandmommy. If Grandmommy is upset, soon everybody will be upset. Grandmommy passes on her moods faster than mosquitoes pass on malaria.

Moji looks up from the computer screen.

"Too Small Tola!" She laughs. "You will fall down when that basket is full!"

Tola tightens her eyes at Moji.

"Don't mind her," Grandmommy says. "I need you to count the change so that

nobody cheats me. Nobody can count faster
than you."

Grandmommy turns back to Moji.

"If Tola is too small, you want to carry the
basket for her?" she asks.

Moji turns back to the computer screen.
Her A+ look deepens.

Grandmommy shakes her head,
but she says nothing.
Tola follows
Grandmommy
out of the apartment,
then pokes her head
back inside.

"Lazy-lazy Moji!"
she shouts, and she
closes the door quickly.
Tola knows that will
make Moji as angry as a
soldier ant.

Grandmommy tiptoes past the other doors. Tola tiptoes behind her. But as soon as they pass the door of Mama Business, it opens.

Mama Business greets them.

"Good morning! Good morning! Where are you going?"

"Good morning, Mama Business," Grandmommy says.

Grandmommy hurries down the dusty concrete steps. Tola hurries behind her.

"You are going to the market?" Mama Business calls.

Grandmommy races out of the crumbling block of apartments. "Now that Mama Mind-Your-Own-Business has seen us, soon everybody will know where we are going."

Dapo looks up from his game.

"Too Small Tola!" he shouts. "That basket is bigger than you!"

Tola's eyes tighten again.

"Don't mind him," Grandmommy says.

She shouts to Dapo, "Do you want to carry it?"

Dapo dribbles the ball very quickly. Grandmommy sucks her teeth.

"Wait until I return!" Grandmommy shouts after him. "Then you will work!"

Dapo pretends not to hear. But Tola can see that he now looks nervous, nervous enough to miss the ball. *Good,* Tola thinks.

Tola follows Grandmommy onto the busy road next to the apartments. The smell of the gutter makes her wrinkle her nose.

She follows Grandmommy under an overpass. The sounds of car horns blaring and hawkers shouting make her wiggle her ears.

She follows Grandmommy past the mall. Tola reads the shop signs: KFC, SAMSUNG, SHOPRITE. Ikeja City Mall has the finest of fine shops. Cold air rushes out of the open doors and makes them shiver.

"Oyinbo air," Grandmommy mutters. "Why did those Tokunbos use juju to bring it here!" She crosses herself.

Tola giggles. Grandmommy thinks that people who have been abroad use magic to bring the cold air back from overseas. But that cold air is just made by air conditioners. Even Tola knows that, Too Small or not!

Tola and Grandmommy cross the lanes of big traffic on the expressway. They walk down busy alleyways where every window opens into a shop and you have to point to what you want. They step over green stinking gutters and squeeze past cars that are crawling along.

It is a long way to Mile 12 Market. But at last they are there! Hundreds of market women shout for people to come and buy their superior goods. Thousands of shoppers scream at the prices of those inferior goods. Tola thinks that Mile 12 Market must be the biggest and busiest place in the whole big and busy city.

Grandmommy sighs happily. She loves Mile 12. Tola sighs too. The long walk has made her tired.

"You are small," Grandmommy says
suddenly, "but you are strong, like me."

Tola looks at Grandmommy in surprise. She
had not realized that Grandmommy was small
too. But now she sees it is true! Grandmommy
is not much taller than her, and that means that
Grandmommy is small. Very small. But Tola
also knows that Grandmommy is very strong.

Grandmommy can pound enough yams
to feed a gathering of the Neighborhood

Association. She can carry enough crates of soft drinks for a birthday party. She can even separate the big Ododi brothers when they are fighting. They do not call Grandmommy Mama Mighty for nothing.

And if Grandmommy is that small but that strong, then maybe Tola can be strong too!

Grandmommy buys huge yams. They are rough and dark on the outside and white and smooth on the inside. After Grandmommy boils and pounds them, eating them will be like eating fluffy white clouds.

Tola counts out the money for the yams. Then she counts the change. Grandmommy loads the heavy-heavy yams into Tola's basket and Tola grunts.

"Too heavy for you?" asks Grandmommy.

"No, Grandmommy," Tola lies.

She is determined to be as strong as Grandmommy.

Grandmommy buys armfuls of leafy green vegetables bursting out of sacks. She buys tiny red chili peppers overflowing from baskets. She buys stiff white stockfish piled into towers.

And each time Tola counts out the money.

She counts the change. Then Grandmommy loads the goods into Tola's basket. Lucky for Tola, they are so light she cannot even feel them.

Grandmommy buys a big sack of rice from the back of a truck loaded with hundreds of sacks.

Tola counts out the money. She counts the change. Then she looks at the big sack of rice.

Grandmommy chuckles.

"I will help you with this one," she says.

The rice seller lifts the sack onto
Grandmommy's head. Grandmommy groans.
"Too heavy for you?" Tola is worried.
"Not at all," Grandmommy lies.

Grandmommy's phone beeps. It is a text from
Dapo. Grandmommy cannot read, so she passes
the phone to Tola.

Tola rolls her
eyes when she
reads the message
out loud. So does
Grandmommy.
But she says,
"O-ya, let us go and
buy it."

"He should come
and carry it," Tola grumbles.
"I will make him sweep the stairs instead,"
says Grandmommy consolingly.

Sweeping the stairs is Tola's job. It is much
more difficult than carrying a light-as-a-chili-
pepper tube of glue. Tola skips a happy little skip.
The basket wobbles.

"You want our shopping to fall in the mud?"
Grandmommy asks.

"No . . ." says Tola, looking down at her muddy feet.
Mile 12 market is always muddy. Even when

it is not the rainy season. And during the rainy season, the whole place turns into one giant muddy puddle. They say that Mile 12 was built on a swamp. As Tola's toes squelch in her flip-flops, she can believe it.

Just then Grandmommy's phone rings. It is Mrs. Abdul from the apartment below.

"Good morning, Mama Mighty," Mrs. Abdul says politely. "I hope that you are well."

"I am well," says Grandmommy.

"I heard that you are in the market," Mrs. Abdul says.

Grandmommy sighs loudly.

"Baby Jide has just used his last diaper," Mrs. Abdul continues.

"What size does he use?" Grandmommy asks in a growly voice.

Mrs. Abdul tells her. And thanks her. And thanks her again. Until Grandmommy ends the call.

Grandmommy buys a package of diapers. Tola counts out the money. She counts the change. Then Grandmommy puts the package of diapers on Tola's head, underneath the basket.

"That should stop you from jumping around," says Grandmommy.

Tola sighs again.

"Something wrong?" asks Grandmommy.

"Nothing, Grandmommy," Tola says. She is determined to be as brave as Grandmommy.

Grandmommy chats with the diaper seller. She tells her all about Moji's grades. The diaper seller reminds Grandmommy that she had predicted Moji would be clever back in the days when Grandmommy was buying diapers for her.

Grandmommy's phone rings again.

"You answer," she says to Tola.

This time it is Moji, crying loudly. Grandmommy snatches the phone.

"What happen? What happen?" shouts Grandmommy.

"It is the mouse!" Tola can hear Moji crying. "I'm having trouble with the mouse! How will I finish my essay?"

"Don't worry!" shouts Grand-mommy. "We will be back soon!"

"There is a mouse in the apartment," Grandmommy explains to Tola. "Your sister is frightened. She cannot finish her homework."

Tola giggles.

"Follow me!" she says to Grandmommy. "I know what we need to buy."

Tola leads Grandmommy through the food market and back into the alleyways. She walks past the plastic shoe sellers, past the bucket sellers, past the fresh meat sellers.

She leads her all the way to the computer sellers.

Tola points to a stall selling just one thing.

"That is what we need," she says.

"Are you sure?" Grandmommy frowns. "I have never chased a mouse with anything like that before."

"I am sure," Tola says. "Moji will not get an A without one."

"OK." Grandmommy sighs.

But when Grandmommy hears the price, she shrieks.

"You want to kill me!" she shouts at the seller. "I need this thing so my granddaughter can get an A. And because of that you want to rob me!"

Grandmommy pretends to walk away until the seller shouts out a more reasonable price. Tola counts out the money. She counts the change.

Then she counts the change again. And again.
She looks at Grandmommy.

"It is short," she whispers.

"Are you sure?" Grandmommy asks.

Tola nods.

Grandmommy takes the change from Tola
and counts it herself.

Then Grandmommy eyes the mouse seller
like a chicken eyeing an ant. The mouse seller
busies himself tidying his stall.

"What is this?" Grandmommy waves the
handful of change under his nose.

"It is your change," the seller says, not looking
at Grandmommy.

"It is short!" Grandmommy growls like a lion.

"It is not short," the man says.

But Tola can see his legs tremble like an
antelope being stalked by a lion. Grandmommy
opens her fist.

"Count!" she demands.

Slowly the mouse seller counts the change.
When he gets to the end, he takes two new
notes from his pocket and adds them to the pile,
then continues counting.

"It is correct," he says.

Grandmommy sucks her teeth. She narrows
her eyes and mutters "tief" under her breath. She
is still grumbling as she tucks the new mouse
into her handbag.

"Too expensive to put into a basket," she says.

Just then Grandmommy's phone rings again.

Grandmommy glares. This time it is old Mr. Obi, calling from one of the top apartments.

"My television needs to be picked up from the repair stall," Mr. Obi croaks.

Grandmommy splutters. She presses a button on the side of the phone. The phone goes dead. Grandmommy looks at the phone. Then she looks at Tola.

"Phone battery done die," Grandmommy says firmly. "I did not hear who was calling."

Tola giggles. Grandmommy nods.

"Enough is enough!" she says firmly. "O-ya, let's go!"

Tola follows Grandmommy through the alleyways.

Grandmommy mutters crossly, "How did he want me to carry it?"

Tola giggles again at the thought of Grandmommy walking along with a television balanced on top of the sack of rice on her head.

"You think it is funny?" she asks. "Maybe he wanted you to carry it. To add to your own tower!"

Tola's eyes widen at the thought of a television added to the package of diapers and the heavy basket on her head.

Tola's face makes Grandmommy laugh.

Tola and Grandmommy laugh together. But they do not laugh for long. Tola's load is very heavy. Grandmommy's load is even heavier.

"We are strong," says Grandmommy. "But we are also small. Let us rest."

Tola and Grandmommy stop in one of the busy alleyways. They rest by a window selling cold soft drinks. They rest and drink well-well, until Grandmommy says,

"O-ya, let's go."

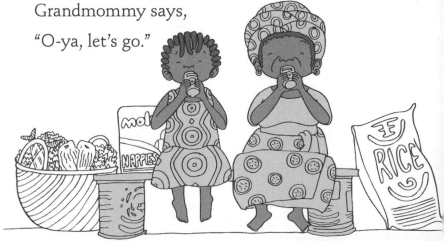

Tola lifts the package of diapers back onto her head. Grandmommy helps her to balance the basket of yams and vegetables and chili peppers and stockfish and the football glue on top. A passerby helps Grandmommy to load the sack of rice back onto her head.

And off they go.

Tola follows Grandmommy closely as they cross the busy expressway. She is afraid of the speeding Mercedes. And the convoys of cars with their screeching horns. And the trucks piled so high with stone and timber that they sag and wobble as if they are about to collapse. Tola sighs hard when they are safely across.

Then Tola follows Grandmommy back past the mall. She reads more shop names—ADIDAS, ISTORE, SILVERBIRD CINEMA.

Grandmommy walks very fast. She does not like oyinbo air at-all, at-all. And she likes juju even less. Tola tries hard to keep up.

But they cannot walk fast
for long. By the time they reach the overpass,
they have slowed right down.

Tola's load is very heavy. Grandmommy's load
is even heavier.

"We are strong," says Grandmommy. "But we
are also small. Let us rest."

So underneath the overpass Tola and Grandmommy rest where the doughnut seller is frying
doughnuts. They rest and eat doughnuts well-
well, until Grandmommy says, "O-ya, let's go."

They lift their loads back onto their heads
and off they go. Now they walk very slowly.
But they cannot even walk slowly for long. By
the time they reach the busy road, Tola stops.

This road leads to the apartments. But they are
still far.

"We are strong," Tola pants, "but we are also
small."

"Let's rest," agrees Grandmommy.

Tola and Grandmommy rest at the ice-cream
seller's bicycle beside the road. They rest and they
eat ice cream well-well, until Grandmommy says,
"O-ya, let's go."

They lift their loads back onto their heads
and off they go. They walk along the busy road.
Now Tola can see the blocks of apartments, and
she knows that they are nearly home. Soon they
see Dapo running toward them.

"Did you buy it? Did you buy it?" Dapo shouts.

Grandmommy eyes him. "Take the rice!"
she barks.

Dapo opens his mouth to argue. Then he looks at Grandmommy's face. Dapo decides to take the rice.

Moji is waiting by their block of apartments.

"Why so long?" she shouts.

"Help your sister with the basket and stop complaining," Grandmommy orders.

Moji looks at Grandmommy's face. She takes the basket from Tola and does not say another word.

Up the stairs they all go. Tola feels as light as a feather with only the diapers to carry.

She starts to sing her favorite D'banj song and shakes her bom-bom up the stairs.

Dapo turns to looks at her.
Moji narrows her eyes.

"Why are you
so happy?" Moji asks.
But Tola is too busy singing
to answer.

"Anyway," says Dapo, "that song is old."

But Tola does not care. She loves it and sings
loudly about Oliver Twist and Beyoncé and
Omotola all the way up.

Inside the flat Grandmommy sits down
heavily on one of the chairs.

"It is good to rest," she says.

"Again," says Tola, giggling.

"What are you laughing about?" asks Dapo.

"Where did you rest before?" Moji asks.

"Nowhere," says Tola.

"Tola," says Grandmommy firmly. "You should not lie to your sister."

"Where did you rest?" shout Moji and Dapo together. "Tell us!"

"Tell them, Tola," says Grandmommy. "You must obey your older siblings."

"OK." Tola grins. "We rested at the soft-drink seller."

"Soft drinks!" Moji and Dapo shout.

"The one in the alleyway near the market," Grandmommy confirms.

"Then we rested at the doughnut seller," Tola continues.

"Doughnuts!" Moji and Dapo shriek.

"The one near the overpass," Grandmommy confirms.

"Finally we rested at the ice-cream seller," Tola says.

"Ice cream!" Moji and Dapo scream.

"The one who cycles up and down the road," Grandmommy confirms.

"Soft drinks, doughnuts, ice cream," Moji wails.

"Did you bring any for us?" Dapo asks hopefully.

Too Small Tola shakes her head. "According to you I am too small to carry much." She grins.

Moji and Dapo groan.

"From now on," Grandmommy says, "you better call her Too Strong Tola."

And Too Strong Tola flexes her small muscles and laughs.

Small but Mighty

Tola lives in a run-down block of apartments in the megacity of Lagos, in the country of Nigeria. Sometimes the electricity works. And sometimes it does not. Sometimes the water runs. And sometimes it does not. Once the elevator worked. And now it definitely does not.

Tola wakes up. She is hot. She is sweating. She can hear Moji snoring in the bed next to her. And she can hear Dapo snoring on the floor. But she cannot hear the ceiling fan whirring around and around.

Tola sighs. The electricity is off. Again.

Tola sits up. It is still dark, but Grandmommy is not in the bed. So she must have already gone to work. It is not time to get up for school, but Tola needs to go to the bathroom.

So she gets up. She creeps out of the bedroom. She tiptoes past Dapo snoring on his mat on the floor.

There is only one room in their apartment. A curtain divides the bedroom part of the room from the part of the room where they cook and sit and study. Room and parlor, Grandmommy calls it.

There is only one bed in the room. Tola and Moji and Grandmommy share the bed. Dapo cannot share it because he is a boy. So he sleeps on a mat on the floor.

Everything in the apartment is battered and old and cheap. Everything except for Grandmommy's earrings. Grandmommy's earrings once belonged to her mother's mother's mother's mother. Grandmommy says that when she wears them she can feel all those mothers blessing her. And that is worth more than the money she could get if she sold those earrings of pure gold.

Tola goes to the bathroom they share with other neighbors. It is a tiny room, with just a toilet and two faucets. When they shower, they take a bucket and position it under the taps. Then they use a jug to pour the water over themselves.

When Tola tries to flush the toilet, it does not flush. She turns on a tap to wash her hands. But no water comes out. Tola sighs again. No electricity. And now no water.

It is one of those mornings when Grandmommy tells them to count their blessings.

"We could be living in the gutter under a cardboard box!" Grandmommy says.

"We could also be living in a big house on Victoria Island," Dapo grumbles.

Big houses all have generators and wells so they always have electricity and water. That is because the people who live there have big money. But Tola's family does not.

Grandmommy works hard selling groundnuts by the road six days a week. She would work seven, but she takes Sundays off to thank God for all of her blessings.

One of her blessings is that Tola's father has a secure job. And he sends the money that pays for the rent of this one room.

"But if only he had a job here in Nigeria and not in the UK," Dapo would complain.

"And what secure job is there in this Nigeria?"

Grandmommy would always ask him.

Tola sighs for the third time. Then she creeps back to the bedroom and pokes Moji.

"Weytin?" Moji asks crossly.

"No water," says Tola.

Moji groans loudly and jumps up.

"O-ya," she says. "Let us go now or we will be late for school."

Tola nods.

She hates to be late for school. Teacher always does math in the morning. And math is her favorite subject.

On the floor Dapo is still snoring. Tola pokes Dapo with her foot. He does not move. Waking up Dapo is like trying to wake a car whose motor has died. No matter what you do, it does not respond.

Dapo is the only person who knows what to do with such a car. If he is not playing football, he is sticking his head into cars to see what makes them work.

"Dapo!" Tola shouts.

Dapo just snores louder. Moji rolls her eyes. She pushes Dapo with her foot. But he just rolls over.

Moji sucks her teeth.

"Come on," she says to Tola. "We don't have time for him."

Under the table are six empty jerry cans waiting for mornings like this when the taps run dry—again.

Moji picks up a jerry can. She balances it on her head.

Tola puts an empty jerry can on her head too. She will fill it. But not to the top. She is not big like Moji.

Tola and Moji have not bothered to change

into their school uniforms. They are going to get
hot and sweaty collecting water. So they just tie
their wrappers tighter.

Then they leave the room and hurry down
the dusty concrete steps. It is still cool outside.
It is still dark. But the
roosters are beginning
to crow and inside the
apartments kerosene
lights are coming on.

"Hurry," says Moji.
"Before everybody else
gets here and we have
to start lining up."

Tola and Moji hurry
to the outside pump.

The taps in the
apartments are connected to water pipes coming
from the government water authority. They
often stop working.

The pump outside the apartments is connected to a borehole that always has water. Water that has to be pumped and then carried up the steep stairs into the apartments.

Moji pumps while Tola positions the jerry cans under the stream of water. When they are full, Tola helps Moji to lift hers onto her head. Moji helps Tola to lift her own.

Then they hurry as fast as they can back to the block of apartments and up the stairs. As fast as they can with their necks aching and their knees buckling and their breaths panting.

They have to collect enough water to flush the toilet. Enough water for Grandmommy to cook with when she comes home. Enough water for her to wash clothes with.

And that means the four empty jerry cans waiting on the floor of the kitchen still need to be filled. And without Dapo's help, they will be late for school. Tola hates being late for school. But Moji hates it even more.

Back in their room Dapo is still snoring. Moji narrows her eyes at him.

"Dapo!" she shouts.

He stops snoring. Then he starts again.

Moji steps up to his mat with the full jerry can still on her head. Tola watches.

Moji stands over Dapo and lifts the full jerry can from her head. Tola stares.

Moji opens the lid of the jerry can and sloshes water onto Dapo's head. Tola snorts.

Dapo leaps from his mat as if it were on fire! He stares around him wildly as if he is being attacked by hidden enemies.

Tola laughs. The jerry can on her own head wobbles, but she cannot stop laughing.

Dapo's eyes focus on Tola. Tola stops laughing. She steps behind Moji. Moji faces Dapo like a tiger facing a crocodile.

"No water," she snaps. "Collect the jerry cans and let's go."

"If no water," Dapo growls, "what did you throw on my head?"

"Jus' help us!" Moji shouts.

"We called you," Tola says, "but you would not wake up."

"I was sleeping!" Dapo shouts. "How could I hear you?"

"Sleeping ko, sleeping ni!" Moji says. "You better hurry up and help us or we will all be late for school."

Dapo grumbles and groans and says that he will complain to Grandmommy, but he picks up two jerry cans. Dapo and Moji rush out. By the time Tola gets to the stairs, they have gone and there is only Mrs. Shaky-Shaky waiting to go down the stairs.

"Good morning, Mrs. Shaky-Shaky," Tola says politely.

"Good morning, Tola," says Mrs. Shaky-Shaky, and she grips Tola's shoulder. Together they go slowly down the stairs.

Mrs. Shaky-Shaky's legs are so shaky she has to grip somebody; otherwise she might fall down.

Now Tola cannot hurry after Moji and Dapo. Now she will be late for school.

Mrs. Shaky-Shaky laughs.

"Look at us, Tola," she says. "We are the same height. Maybe, like me, you will stay small."

Tola looks at Mrs. Shaky-Shaky. It is true. They are exactly the same height! This means that some people never grow any taller. And maybe one of those people is Tola!

"Don't let anyone tell you that you are too small," Mrs. Shaky-Shaky says as they reach the bottom of the stairs. "One can never be too small."

"No, Ma," says Tola sadly, knowing it is not true.

Mrs. Shaky-Shaky smiles. She pinches Tola's cheek with a shaky hand.

"You are a good girl, Tola," she says. "Thank you for your help.

Now run or you will be late for school."

So Tola runs. But by the time she reaches the pump there is a long line of people waiting with buckets and jars and jerry cans. Moji and Dapo are near the front.

"What is wrong with you?" Moji shouts at Tola when she takes her place at the back. "Now you will be late!"

One of the troublesome Ododi brothers joins the line behind Tola. He heard what Moji shouted.

"What is wrong with her? What is wrong?" he shouts back. "She's Too Small Tola! That's what is wrong with her!"

He laughs. And other people in the line laugh too.

Tola presses her lips together. But she does not say anything. Nobody messes with the Ododi boys. Not even people bigger than her.

"Sorry, Tola," Moji whispers when she goes past with her full jerry cans.

Tola does not look at Moji. She does not answer her. If she did, she would cry. So she just keeps her eyes on the ground all the way to the pump. She has to work the heavy pump all by herself. Then she struggles to lift the heavy jerry can onto her head.

"Look at Too Small Tola!" the Ododi boy shouts. "So small she is practically useless."

Tola tries hard not to cry. But nobody laughs this time. Mrs. Ronke steps forward to help Tola lift the can onto her head. But nobody says anything to the Ododi boy. Nobody messes with the Ododi brothers.

Tola turns back toward the apartments and starts to walk. Her neck is aching, her knees are buckling, and she is panting.

And just as she passes the Ododi boy, Tola trips. She feels herself falling. The jerry can hits the ground and the lid comes off. Water pours out onto the ground.

Tola hears the Ododi boy laugh. She sits up. The Ododi boy has his foot sticking out into the path. He tripped Tola! He tripped her up on purpose!

Mrs. Shaky-Shaky is standing in the line on her shaky-shaky legs. She looks at Tola but she does not say anything. Nobody in the line says anything. Nobody messes with the Ododi brothers.

Tola picks up her almost-empty jerry can and joins the back of the line again. She is crying now. Crying because she is so angry. And she does not even care that everybody can see her cry.

It is the Ododi boy's turn to fill his buckets. When he is done he turns back toward the flats. There is a big jeering smile on his face as he looks at Tola.

But just as he passes Mrs. Shaky-Shaky, the Ododi boy trips. He lands on the ground hard. His buckets empty themselves.

People jump back and shriek as the water splashes them. Then the whole line goes silent.

Everyone stares at the Ododi boy lying on the ground.

Then they stare at Mrs. Shaky-Shaky's foot stuck out on the path.

Slowly people start to clap. They clap for the tiny, shaky old lady who felled the big, tough, troublesome boy.

Tola stares. She stares at the small-small lady who took down the big bad boy just for her. Tola stops crying.

The Ododi boy leaps to his feet. He looks at Mrs. Shaky-Shaky with her foot sticking out. Then he stands over Mrs. Shaky-Shaky and bunches his fists.

Tola leaps forward. She leaps in front of Mrs. Shaky-Shaky to shield her from the Ododi boy's fists.

Then Tola sees old Mrs. Ebiri, who is as tough as stockfish, step forward. And huge Mrs. Raheen, who once took down an armed robber with a yam pounder. And tiny Mrs. Ambode, who kills giant rats with only a broom.

Tola closes her eyes. She closes her eyes tight-tight-tight so that she cannot see his big-big fists and his angry-angry face.

With her eyes closed, Tola sees nothing. But she knows that something is going to happen. There is a good reason that nobody messes with the Ododi brothers. Tola is trembling. But she does not run. She cannot leave Mrs. Shaky-Shaky to be knocked down.

For some time nothing happens. Tola can see nothing. Tola can hear nothing. Eventually she takes a little peek.

Standing on one side of her is fat Mama Kunle. She must have left her place in the line. On the other side is Mrs. Abdul with baby Jide strapped to her back. They must have left their places in the line too.

They all leave their places in the line and stand beside Tola and Mrs. Shaky-Shaky.

Tola dares to look at the Ododi boy then. His eyes are flitting from one woman to another. Tiny Mrs. Ambode takes one step forward.

And the Ododi boy steps back.

Mrs. Shaky-Shaky pokes her shaky head around Tola.

"You are afraid of an old lady?" she asks. "Come on!" she says, doubling up her shaky-shaky fists.

Mrs. Raheen rolls up her sleeves. And Mrs. Ebiri unties her headscarf and ties it around her waist. Mama Kunle positions her legs wider. The women are ready to fight! The Ododi boy takes another step back.

Suddenly he turns and runs!

Mrs. Shaky-Shaky starts to laugh. She laughs and laughs and all the women join in.

"If you try anything again," Mrs. Shaky-Shaky shouts after the Ododi boy, "you will have me to reckon with!"

And she waves her shaky-shaky fists.

All the women laugh again. Then they readjust their clothing, pick up their buckets and jars and jerry cans, and resume their places in the line.

Mrs. Shaky-Shaky pinches Tola's cheek with a shaky hand.

"Remember what I told you," she says. "There is no such

thing as too small. And you are mighty. Just like your grandmother."

Tola rubs her cheek. She stares at the small figure of the Ododi brother, who is still running. Did she really help to scare him away?

Then Tola hears someone calling her name. It is Dapo. He is hurrying toward her, carrying the last two jerry cans.

"Give me your can," he says. "I will fill it for you."

Tola hands him the can.

"Now run!" Dapo says. "Or you will be late for school."

Tola smiles. She smiles at Mrs. Shaky-Shaky. And she smiles at Dapo.

"Thank you!" she says, and then she runs.

Tola runs back to the apartment. She fills a bucket half full with water from one of the full jerry cans. She carries the bucket and some black soap and a towel to the bathroom.

She uses a jug to pour water over herself, uses the soap to wash herself, and uses the rest of the water to rinse herself. She dries herself with the towel and goes back to the room.

Moji is just leaving. She is wearing her smart white-and-blue striped uniform with her tie. She is wearing a backpack and smart shining shoes. In her hand she has a slice of bread.

"There is bread and sardines on the table for you," she says as she bangs the door behind her.

Tola struggles into her uniform. It is not smart like Moji's. It is plain and brown. And she does not have smart shoes, just her old flip-flops. But she does not have a scholarship to help her go to a fancy school. Not like Moji.

Tola tries to ignore the bread and sardines so that she is not late. But she is too hungry. So she stuffs some into her mouth. Then she snatches up her bag and rushes out the door.

On the stairs she passes Dapo. He has one jerry can on his head and two in his hands. With every step he has to stop and put down the cans he is carrying. Sweat is running down his face.

Tola looks at Dapo. She sighs. Then she points to one of the jerry cans and points to her head. Her mouth is too stuffed full of bread and sardines to speak. Dapo shakes his head.

"Jus' go!" he says.

So Tola goes. Dapo does not care about missing school. But she does. And he knows that. Tola will run all the way, but Dapo will linger, kicking a ball to any boy who is around, and poking his head into the engine of any car that has its hood open.

Tola runs down the stairs. She runs out
the door. She runs across the rough ground to
the road. There are many rusty yellow danfo
minibuses juddering along.

One stops. It is already jammed with people.
But Tola squeezes in. The danfo starts with a
jerk. It chugs off down the road. Soon they are
at the street of Tola's school.

Tola jumps off the bus and runs up the street.
She does not know if she is late or not. She does
not have a phone, or even a watch. She runs
to the school building and into her class.

The teacher is standing beside his desk. Children are crammed around tables in front of him.

"Tola Adebayo!" the teacher calls.

"Yes, sa!" Tola answers. She is in trouble now.

But then the teacher calls another name. Tola sighs with relief. Teacher is just taking attendance!

Tola slips onto her chair. She smiles at her friend who sits next to her. She is not late. Not even one minute late! So she has missed no math at all!

Easter and Eid

Tola lives in a run-down block of apartments
in the megacity of Lagos, in the country of
Nigeria.

Soon it will be both Easter and the end of
the Ramadan feast of Eid. Everybody in the
apartments is happy. Easter and Eid do not
often happen at the same time, and celebrations
are all anybody is talking about.

"I am planning our Eid feast," says Mrs. Abdul hungrily.

Mrs. Abdul fasts during Ramadan and gives the money she usually spends on food to the homeless.

"And I am looking forward to shaking my palm leaves in the procession on Palm Sunday," says Mrs. Shaky-Shaky.

"Me too!" says Tola.

"It will be a beautiful sight," agrees Mrs. Abdul.

Tola is so looking forward to Easter. The whole family gets new clothes for Easter Sunday.

And they process through the streets to church, waving their palm leaves and singing. It is always a wonderful day.

Tola and Grandmommy are busy planning their outfits. Tola wants ruffles on hers, but Grandmommy shakes her head. Ruffles take a lot of time to make, so they cost more money than Grandmommy has got. Tola sighs. She has never had ruffles. And she has always wanted them.

Moji is bent over her schoolwork. And Dapo is complaining—as usual.

"How can I become a professional footballer," he moans, "without professional training?"

Tola, Moji, and Grandmommy try to ignore him. They wish that he would be quiet. But Dapo has been moaning for weeks, and he is not going to stop now.

"How am I supposed to train without a coach?" he wails.

"Maybe you are good enough without training," says Tola.

Dapo opens his mouth to reply. But there is a knock on the door. It is Mr. Abdul, the tailor.

"Salam alekum," Mr. Abdul says politely.

"Peace be with you too," Grandmommy says. "Come in, come in," she gestures.

Mr. Abdul looks at Dapo, who has his head in his hands.

"That boy's muscles get bigger every time I see him," Mr. Abdul says.

Dapo lifts his head. He smiles proudly.

Mr. Abdul looks at Moji squinting at her screen.

"And this one is on her way to being a doctor, I hear," he says.

Moji looks up. She actually takes the time to smile too.

Mr. Abdul looks at Tola, jumping up and down behind Grandmommy.

"And you are the little one who likes to count, are you not?" Mr. Abdul asks.

Tola nods shyly. She smiles. Numbers are her favorite thing.

Last year Mr. Abdul let her use his tape measure when he came to measure the family for their Easter outfits. Tola had measured everybody's waists and shoulders. And she had gotten most of the measurements right.

"Do you want to measure today?" Mr. Abdul asks.

Tola nods again.

Mr. Abdul hands her his tape measure.

"Go ahead," he says.

Dapo laughs. Moji raises her eyebrows.

But Tola just ignores them.

"Don't pull the tape too tight," Mr. Abdul
reminds her as she is measuring Grandmommy's
arms.

"Don't let the tape hang slack," he says as she
is measuring Moji's long legs.

"Don't forget around those arms," he adds as
she is measuring Dapo's broad shoulders.

Tola carefully writes down each and every
measurement on a piece of paper. And then
Mr. Abdul measures exactly what she has just
measured.

And each and every measurement is exactly
the same!

Mr. Abdul looks at Tola in amazement.

"Tola! Tola!" he says. "This is wonderful. You
must be the best measurer in Lagos!"

Dapo looks astonished. Moji looks startled.
But Grandmommy nods as if she knew. Tola
smiles shyly.

Then Mr. Abdul turns to Grandmommy. "You
have chosen the cloth?"

Grandmommy has. She has chosen green cloth
with purple butterflies from the market. All their
outfits will be made from the same cloth.

"Butterflies!" Tola had clapped her hands when
she had seen it.

"I would have preferred BMWs," Dapo had
complained.

Moji had said nothing. The only butterflies she
noticed were the equations fluttering around in
her head.

"Beautiful, beautiful," Mr. Abdul says when he sees it. "You will all look very fine."

Mr. Abdul goes off with the cloth and the measurements inside his head. He will sew their clothes in his apartment downstairs. That is where he makes all his customers' clothes. And when they are ready he will return with them.

Tola looks out of the window and sees him cycling off to see another customer, his sewing machine strapped to the back of his big bicycle.

Mr. Abdul always takes his sewing machine with him, just in case he has to do repairs or adjustments for his customers.

But when Tola comes home from school the next day, there is bad news.

"An okada motorbike overtook Mr. Abdul," Grandmommy says. "He fell off his bicycle and broke his leg."

Tola gasps and claps her hand over her mouth.

"Luckily," Grandmommy continues, "the sewing machine was not damaged."

Tola is glad. At least with his sewing machine Mr. Abdul can still work.

When Tola and Grandmommy go downstairs to visit Mr. Abdul, he is sitting cheerfully on the floor in front of his sewing machine. He is busy sewing green cloth with purple butterflies!

"Our clothes!" says Tola.

"Of course." Mr. Abdul smiles. "I do not allow broken legs to spoil Easter!"

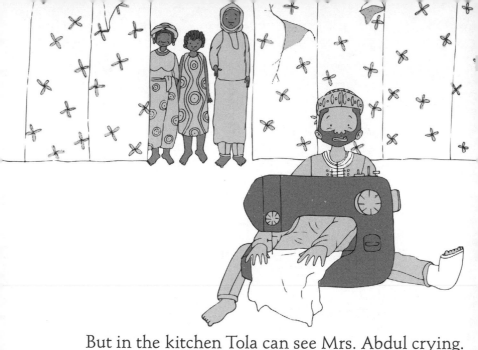

But in the kitchen Tola can see Mrs. Abdul crying.
"Those okada drivers!" she wails. "They are too-
too dangerous! The governor keeps saying they are
banned, but they are still everywhere. Everywhere!
Now what will we do, Mama Mighty? What will
we do?"

Grandmommy goes to comfort her. They talk for
a long time.

"Mr. Abdul can still make clothes," Grandmommy
explains later, "but he cannot ride his bike around

the city to take orders from his customers."

"Is that why Mrs. Abdul was crying?" asks Tola.

"Shh!" says Moji. "I am trying to study."

Grandmommy ignores Moji.

"Yes," she says. "Mr. Abdul's customers will have to get another tailor. And Mr. Abdul will lose money."

"What about their Ramadan feast?" Tola asks.

Feasts cost money. Tola knows that.

"Shh!" says Moji again.

But Tola is too worried about Mr. and Mrs. Abdul to take any notice.

"They cannot miss their feast!" Tola cries. "They have been fasting for weeks!"

"Worse than that." Grandmommy is worried. "They might not be able to pay the rent."

"Oh no!" cries Tola.

"Be quiet, Tola!" shouts Moji.

"But, Mr. Abdul!" Tola shouts back.

"If you are so worried about Mr. Abdul, why don't you go and measure his customers yourself!" Moji says crossly.

Dapo laughs.

"Can you imagine?" he says. "Too Small Tola trying to ride that bicycle!"

Tola narrows her eyes at him. Dapo laughs even louder.

"I can see it now!" he snorts. "Those small-small legs trying to reach the pedals!"

"If you think it is so funny, then maybe you should ride the bicycle!" Tola shouts angrily. She punches his arm.

Dapo stops laughing. He rubs his arm.

"Did you see what she did to me?" he complains to Grandmommy.

Grandmommy says nothing. She looks at Tola, then she looks at Dapo. Then she looks back at Tola and rubs her fat hands together.

"Uh-oh!" says Dapo.

"It is a good idea," Grandmommy announces. "Tola can measure the customers. Dapo can ride the bicycle."

Tola stares at Grandmommy. *What?*

"What!" shouts Dapo. "I am not pedaling around and around on that heavy bicycle."

"Think of it as training," Grandmommy says, smiling.

"It's what you have always wanted." Moji smirks.

Tola giggles then too.

Dapo opens his mouth to argue.

"Think how big your calf muscles will grow," Grandmommy continues.

"It will be just like going to the gym," Moji joins in. "All day long."

"Oh no!" Dapo groans. "All the other boys will laugh at me."

Tola giggles again.

Then she thinks of herself on the back of that bike. And she thinks of all those strangers, all those strangers Grandmommy wants her to measure.

Tola stops giggling.

But when Grandmommy tells Mr. Abdul the idea, and when he looks at Tola, and when he asks, "You will do this? You will do this for me?" then Tola remembers Mrs. Abdul crying. And she remembers how

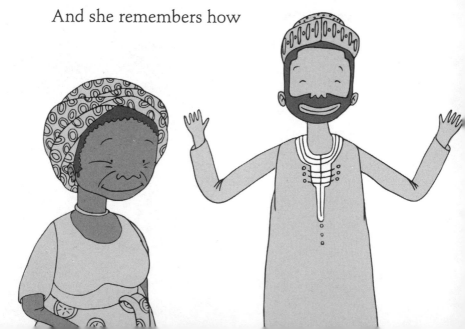

Mr. Abdul is kind to everybody. So she takes a deep breath. And she nods.

"I am a lucky man!" Mr. Abdul proclaims. "I have the best measurer in all of Lagos taking my measurements!"

And Tola manages a tiny-tiny smile.

Then Mr. Abdul looks at Dapo.

"And with you in charge of my bike," he says, "it will be reaching record speeds."

Then Dapo manages a smile too.

Mr. Abdul explains to Tola all about his customers—the fussy ones, the kind ones, the grumpy ones. Those who would offer them water and those who would only complain.

Then Mr. Abdul explains to Dapo about how to find all those customers. Those that live at the top of apartments as tall as giraffes. Those who live at the bottom of alleyways that smell like hyenas. Those who live in mansions the size of a whole herd of elephants.

Then Tola takes the measuring tape and a
small bit of paper and an even smaller bit of pencil
from Mr. Abdul. And Dapo and Tola get onto
Mr. Abdul's big bicycle.
And off they go.

Grandmommy waves goodbye.

"Do a good job!" she shouts to Tola. "Look after
your sister!" she shouts to Dapo.

Dapo pedals the bicycle along the bumpy road.
There are potholes full of water and mud and
stones. There are cars bumper to bumper honking
their horns. Tola holds on tight.

Dapo stops at a small clean block of apartments.

Outside it there is grass and big trees giving shade and flowers in pots. Tola stares. It looks nothing like their crumbling block of apartments with its stained walls and the rough potholed bare earth around it.

A lady waves to them from a balcony.

"Enter! Enter!" she says. "Mr. Abdul called to say that you were coming."

The lady offers them soft drinks. Then she and her five children line up.

Tola measures the lady and writes down her measurements. She measures the five children and writes down each and every one of their measurements. Mr. Abdul would not have had to write anything down. Mr. Abdul cannot write. But his memory is as long as an elephant's trunk.

Tola collects the drawings of the outfits that the lady wants. And the lady gives her the cloth that she wants the outfits to be made from.

And then they get back onto Mr. Abdul's bike.

The lady and her children wave goodbye.

"Thank you! Thank you!" they shout. "We look forward to our new Eid clothes."

Dapo pedals away. Tola holds on tight. They cross the huge Third Mainland Bridge with its eight official lanes of traffic. It is the second longest bridge in Africa. Tola knows that from school.

Then Dapo pedals down the rocky, bumpy streets of Ikoyi. Here the gutters do not smell. And on either side of them are high walls topped with broken glass.

Dapo stops at some metal gates with a tiny intercom. The gates open by themselves to let them in.

Inside is a house as big as an oba's palace. It has shining white walls and thick white pillars holding up its balconies. A uniformed man comes out. He looks down at Dapo's dusty bare feet. He looks at Too Small Tola. Then he raises his eyebrows.

Tola pokes Dapo.

"Good morning," Dapo says. "We are Mr. Abdul's assistants."

"Madam will only see Mr. Abdul," the man replies.

"OK," Dapo says, and he starts to turn the bike around.

Tola pokes Dapo even harder.

Dapo sighs and says, "Mr. Abdul has sent the best measurer in Lagos to measure her."

The uniformed man frowns. Then he marches back inside the house.

"Can we go now?" Dapo asks.

Tola shakes her head.

After a while a very fancy woman comes out. She is wearing fine clothes and heavy gold jewelry, and her feet are spilling out over tiny-tiny shoes. She glares at Dapo and Tola.

"Before you touch me," she says, "you must wash your hands."

Dapo opens his mouth to argue. Tola pokes him again.

She gets off the bicycle. She washes her hands carefully at the garden tap. Then she measures the woman. She writes the measurements down. The woman calls her servant to bring out some magazines. She shows Tola two pictures of what she wants her outfit to look like.

"Like this?" Tola points at the sleeves in one of the pictures. "Or like this?" She points at the sleeves in the other picture.

"No! No!" the woman shouts.

She turns the pages and shows Tola a different picture altogether. Tola places a check beside the sleeves in the third picture.

"Like this?" Tola points at the skirt in the first picture. "Or like this?" She points at the skirt in the second picture.

"No! No!" the woman shouts.

She turns the pages and shows Tola yet another picture. Tola places a check beside the skirt in the fourth picture.

"Like this?" Tola points at the neckline in the first picture. "Or like this?" She points at the neckline in the second picture.

"No! No!" the woman shouts.

She turns the pages and points to the neckline in a fifth picture. Tola places a check beside it.

It takes a long time and a lot of pictures until at last Tola thinks she knows exactly what the woman wants her outfit to look like. Tola wants to be sure that she makes no mistakes.

Dapo stands by the bike and scowls.

"Make sure you get it right!" the woman shouts, pushing the magazine at Tola, "or I will not pay!"

Tola nods. She gets back onto the bike with the magazine. And off they go.

When the big metal gates close behind them, Dapo says some words that Grandmommy has banned. Tola grins.

Now they have to go to Victoria Island. Dapo pedals down streets that are almost empty of cars. Instead there are shady trees. Tola cranes her neck and looks up. In the branches of the trees, birds sing and monkeys screech. She smiles. It is good to be away from the loud, smelly traffic and the hot-hot sun.

Dapo stops at a house made of glass and metal. It is not like a house, Tola thinks. It is more like a shop showing off every fine-fine thing inside. Parked beside the house is a Lamborghini, a Porsche, and a Jeep.

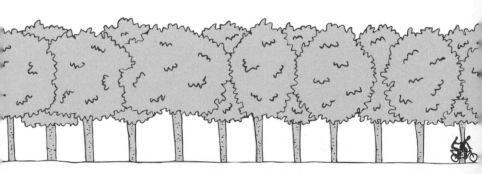

Dapo parks the bike next to the cars and stares and stares and stares. Next to football, Dapo likes cars best.

Afrobeat music blares out as soon as the front door opens. A man and a woman come out. The woman is wearing clothes so tight and shoes so high that her legs seem as long as a giraffe's. And the man's trousers are so low that his legs seem as short as a tortoise's.

Tola looks at them with her mouth open until the man coughs and Tola remembers why she is there.

"Tell Mr. Abdul we want totally traditional outfits this time," the woman says. "Ankara for both of us."

Tola nods in time to the music. Even her shoulders nod. She cannot help herself. She loves Afrobeat.

"You like it?" The man laughs.

Tola's body is still nodding.

"It is my tune," the man says, as if it was nothing.

This time Tola's mouth opens and closes in time to the music. This tune is famous! This man is famous! The man laughs.

"Measure me!" He laughs, opening his arms. "And I will sign your measurements."

Tola can't help clapping her hands. And Dapo

dances around the cars. The music has taken his body, but his mind is still on those fine-fine cars.

At last they have measured every single person on Mr. Abdul's list. Back they go along the shady roads of Victoria Island. Back along the bumpy roads of Ikoyi. Back over the Third Mainland Bridge with its more-than-eight unofficial lanes of cars and trucks and taxis and buses and limousines and motorbikes and minibuses and tankers and motorcades. Back past the bumper-to-bumper traffic of mainland Lagos. All the long hot way home.

When they get there, Tola runs into Mr. Abdul's room and parlor with all the cloth and all the measurements.

Mr. Abdul claps his hands happily to see them. Tola shows him the measurements and he smiles. She shows him the magazine pictures and tells him what each customer wants and he nods.

She hands him the cloth.

Then Mr. Abdul gets out his scissors.

"Are you sure, *habibi*?" Mrs. Abdul asks, worried. "Are you sure the measurements are right?"

Tola looks worried then too. But Mr. Abdul nods.

"I am as sure as sure can be," he says. "Tola's measurements are as good as my measurements."

Tola crosses all her fingers and all her toes.

Now every day Tola and Dapo ride around the city visiting shacks and chalets, mansions and markets, houses and hotels.

Dapo pedals

and pedals

and pedals. Tola measures

and measures

and measures.

And back at the apartments Mr.
Abdul sews and sews and sews.

Then, just before
Easter and the end of
Ramadan, Tola and Dapo
deliver all the clothes.

Tola's fingers are crossed so tightly that her
hands ache. Her toes are crossed so tightly that
her feet hurt. She is so nervous that even her
stomach is crossed in a knot!

She watches and waits as each
and every customer tries on each
and every outfit. And all the outfits
fit! Each and every one fits perfectly.

Even the large and fancy woman cannot complain.

Tola collects money from all of Mr. Abdul's customers. And from the large and fancy woman she collects more than ten times as much money. Mr. Abdul had warned Tola about that woman from the beginning. And he had told her what to charge her at the end. It was the price of rudeness, he said.

When they hand over the money to Mr. Abdul, Mrs. Abdul is so happy she cries and hugs them, and cries and hugs them again.

Tola and Dapo are happy too. Dapo's calf muscles are as big as the pillars holding up the Third Mainland Bridge. Tola's memory for measurements is as long as the lines of traffic that cross it. And most importantly, Mr. and

Mrs. Abdul have all the money that they need for their rent and for their Ramadan feast!

On Easter Sunday, Tola and her family will parade all the way to church with their palm leaves. And in the evening they will go to Mr. and Mrs. Abdul's end-of-Ramadan Eid feast. It will be a wonderful day.

Mr. Abdul finishes Tola's new Easter outfit. He holds it up for her to see. Tola gasps and covers her mouth. All over her new Easter outfit are ruffles. The tiniest, cutest ruffles she has ever-ever seen!